For Steve and Julie

Text and illustrations copyright © 1993 by Hilda Offen

All rights reserved.

CIP Data is available.

First published in the United States 1993
by Dutton Children's Books,
a division of Penguin Books USA Inc.
375 Hudson Street, New York, New York 10014
Originally published in Great Britain 1993
by Hamish Hamilton Ltd., London
Display typography by Makiko Ushiba
Printed in Hong Kong
FIRST AMERICAN EDITION
ISBN 0-525-45123-4

1 3 5 7 9 10 8 6 4 2

ELEPHANT
PIE by Hilda Offen

DUTTON CHILDREN'S BOOKS · NEW YORK

What would you like for your birthday, my dearest dear?" asked Mr. Snipper-Snapper.

"A party!" said Mrs. Snipper-Snapper. "And a cherry pie with lots and lots of custard!" She was so excited that she burst into tears. *Splish! Splash!* The Snipper-Snappers were very tearful crocodiles.

Mr. Snipper-Snapper ran to fetch the mop. Then he called Mrs. Elephant, the best pie baker in town, to order the pie.

Ting-a-ling-a-ling! Mrs. Elephant answered the phone and took the order. "The Snipper-Snappers want a birthday pie!" she told her children.

"Please let me help!" said Edward.

"No, Edward!" said his mother. "You mix things up. The last time, you put a pinch of pepper in the pastry instead of salt."

Mrs. Elephant fetched a bowl of cherries from the refrigerator.

"Want some!" said baby Jojo.

"Not now, Jojo!" said Mrs. Elephant. "Go and play with your building blocks."

Mrs. Elephant rolled the pastry. She made the pie in her biggest dish and popped it in the oven.

When the pie was baked, Mrs. Elephant set it on the table to cool. Then she decorated it with pink icing, candy roses, and candles. "Now, I have to do the laundry," she said. Edward went along to help.

When they came back into the kitchen, Jojo had disappeared.

Naughty Jojo! Where could she be? They looked in the cupboards—no Jojo.

They looked under the beds— no Jojo.

They looked in the laundry basket—no Jojo.
Mrs. Elephant was frantic!

"Oh dear, could Jojo have wandered out of the
yard? Oh dear, Edward, you'll have to deliver the
pie! Oh dear, oh dear, the Snipper-Snappers
wanted custard, too."

But Mrs. Elephant was so flustered, she made
the custard out of mustard.

"Mom!" said Edward. "You've made a mistake!"

But Mrs. Elephant was too upset to listen.

She loaded the pie into the wheelbarrow and put the jug of custard into Edward's backpack. "Keep a lookout for your sister!" she said. Then she ran up the lane, calling, "Jojo! Jojo!"

Edward set off with the wheelbarrow. "Jojo!" he called. "Where are you?"

"We've seen her up that pine tree!" shrieked some parrots.

Edward went to look. While he was gone, the parrots pecked all the candles off the pie. Then they flew away.

"Jojo!" called Edward as he went past the woods. A bear ran out from the trees.

"I've seen her near the pond," it said.

Edward went to look. While he was gone, the bear ate all the candy roses. Then it ran away.

Edward came to a field. "Jojo!" he called. A donkey leaned over the hedge.

"I've seen her in that ditch!" it said.

Edward went to look.

While he was gone, the donkey nibbled the edges of the piecrust. Then it galloped off.

The pie looked terrible. Perhaps the Snipper-Snappers won't notice, said Edward to himself. He trundled the wheelbarrow up to their front door and knocked.

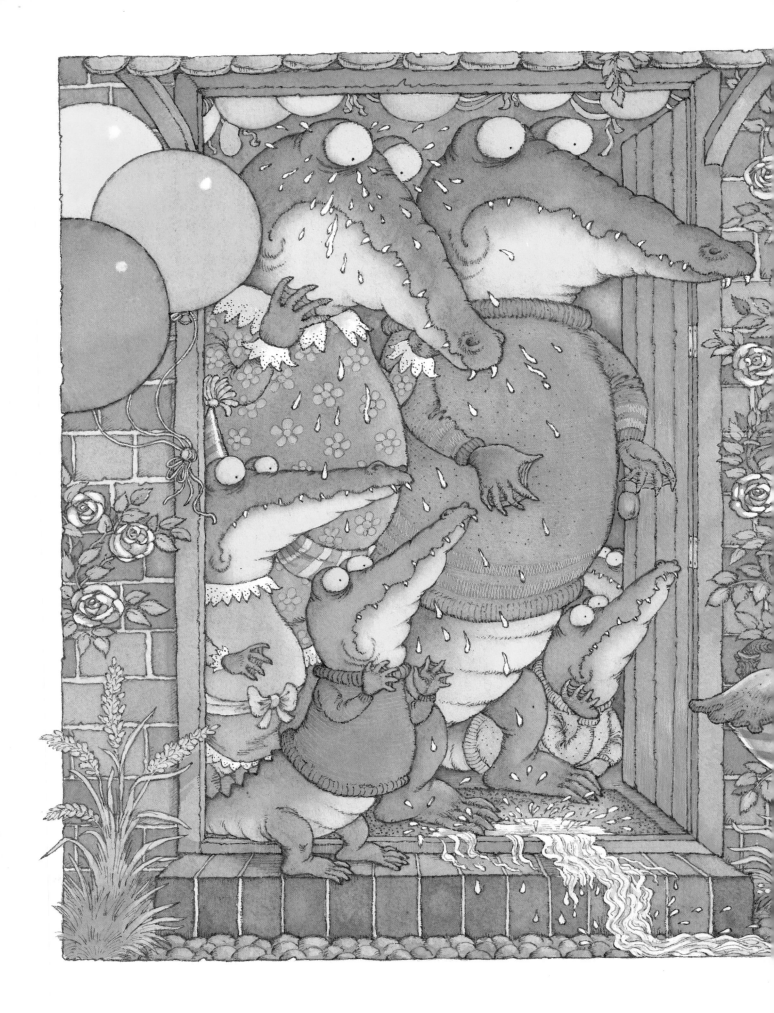

The Snipper-Snappers opened the door.

"Your pie!" said Edward.

Mr. Snipper-Snapper stared. Mrs. Snipper-Snapper stared. The Aunties and the Uncles and all the little Snipper-Snappers stared.

"This?" cried Mrs. Snipper-Snapper. "This is my birthday pie?"

She began to sob. Her tears splashed onto the doorstep and trickled down the path.

Mr. Snipper-Snapper snatched the pie and slammed the door in Edward's face.

"Boo-hoo!" sobbed Mrs. Snipper-Snapper. "Boo-hoo!" wailed the Aunties and the Uncles. "Boo-hoo!" roared the little Snipper-Snappers. What a noise!

Jojo, who had fallen fast asleep, opened her eyes. She yawned. She stretched.

The piecrust began to crack!

"Oh!" gasped the Snipper-Snappers as Jojo burst out of the pie.

"Wahhh!" screamed Jojo. "I want my mom!"

When Edward heard his sister's voice, he ran back up the path and peeked through the window. There was Jojo—sitting in the pie dish! And he saw the Snipper-Snappers crowding around and clicking their terrible teeth.

"Never mind the cherries, my dear!" he heard Mr. Snipper-Snapper say. "We'll have elephant pie instead."

Oh no! thought Edward. What should I do? Then he had an idea. "Don't you want your custard?" he called.

"The custard! The custard!" squealed all the Snipper-Snappers. Mrs. Snipper-Snapper snatched the jug from Edward and tipped it over Jojo's head. *Slippety-slop!* Down poured the custard, over Jojo's ears, over her tummy, and into the pie dish.

"Mmm!" said Mrs. Snipper-Snapper. "We love custard!"

She leaned forward and took a big lick. All the other Snipper-Snappers did the same.

"Aargh!" they shrieked as the mustard in the custard burned their tongues.

Tears sprang to the Snipper-Snappers' eyes and poured to the floor. Soon they were knee-deep in water. "Boo-hoo!" they howled. "Boo-hoo!" Their tongues were on fire! The more they cried, the higher the water rose. It reached the tabletop— and away floated Jojo in the pie dish, across the room and out the window!

Edward put her in the wheelbarrow and ran. He ran and he
ran and he didn't stop
running until he
reached home.

Mrs. Elephant was overjoyed to see her baby safe and sound.

"Thank you, Edward!" she said.

She gave Jojo a bath and washed off all the mustard custard. Then she tucked her into bed.

But she let Edward stay up late. And she let him make a pie of his very own. It was a strawberry pie, with whipped cream on top. They had it for supper.

"It's a perfect pie!" said Mrs. Elephant. "The best pie I've ever tasted!"